People at Work

Working at a Fire Station

by Connor Stratton

FOCUS READERS®

SCOUT

www.focusreaders.com

Focus Readers is distributed by North Star Editions:
sales@northstareditions.com | 888-417-0195

Produced for Focus Readers by Red Line Editorial.

Photographs ©: kali9/iStockphoto, cover, 1; Manuel Esteban/Shutterstock Images, 4 (top); Pavel L Photo and Video/Shutterstock Images, 4 (bottom); Lpettet/iStockphoto, 7 (top); poco_bw/iStockphoto, 7 (bottom); praisaeng/iStockphoto, 9 (top), 16 (top right); shaunl/iStockphoto, 9 (bottom); davelogan/iStockphoto, 11; gorodenkoff/iStockphoto, 13; Mordolff/iStockphoto, 15; kudou/iStockphoto, 16 (top left); Shoot First Media Atlanta/Shutterstock Images, 16 (bottom left); sergeyryzhov/iStockphoto, 16 (bottom right)

Library of Congress Cataloging-in-Publication Data
Library of Congress Cataloging-in-Publication Data is available on the Library of Congress website.

ISBN
978-1-64493-014-4 (hardcover)
978-1-64493-093-9 (paperback)
978-1-64493-251-3 (ebook pdf)
978-1-64493-172-1 (hosted ebook)

Printed in the United States of America
Mankato, MN
012020

About the Author

Connor Stratton enjoys learning new things, eating popcorn, and watching movies with friends. He lives in Minnesota.

Table of Contents

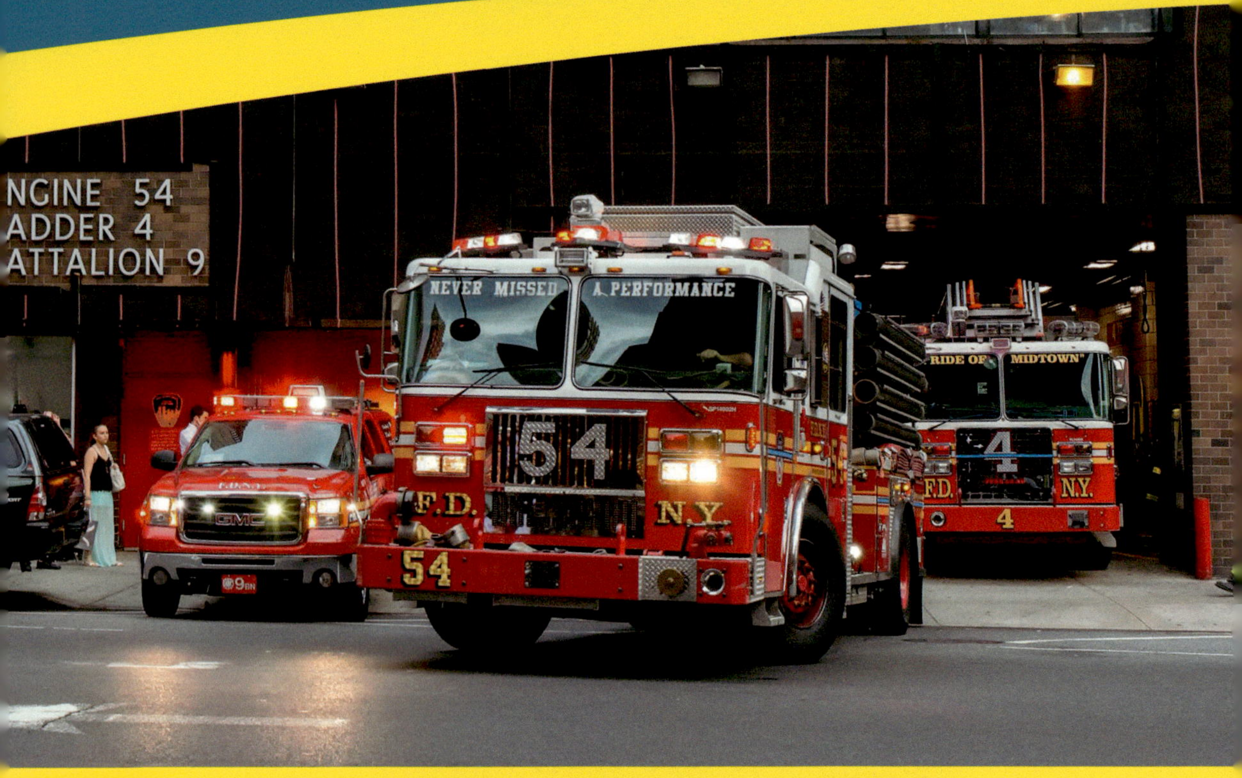

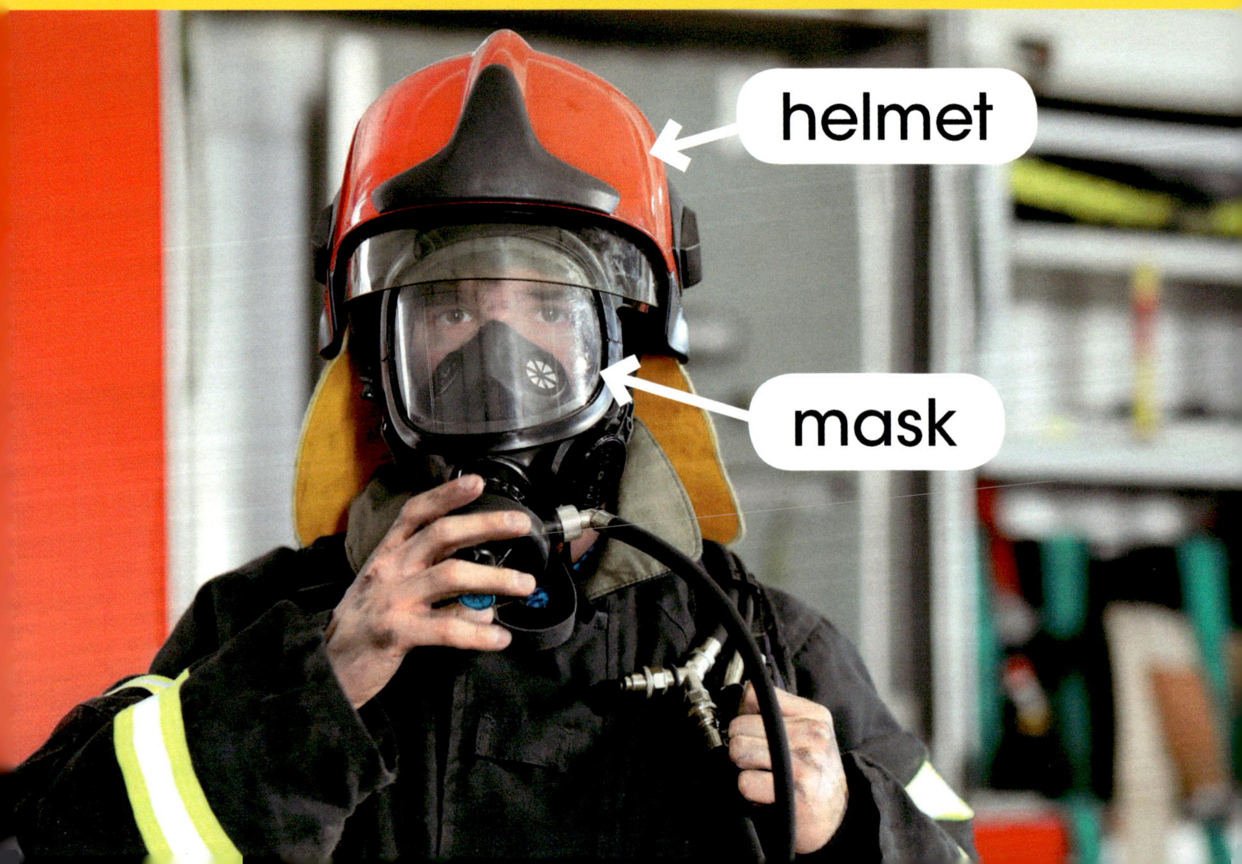

helmet

mask

Firefighters

Firefighters work at the
fire station.
They put on **helmets**.
They put on **masks**.

Firefighters drive to the fire.

They drive in a fire truck.

fire truck

Putting Out Fires

Firefighters use a **hose**.

The hose shoots water.

hose

water

Firefighters work together.

They put out the fire.

Helping People

Firefighters go into the fire.

They use **flashlights**.

Flashlights help

firefighters see.

flashlight

Firefighters carry people.

Firefighters save people.

Glossary

flashlights

hose

helmets

masks

Index